For my darling Gabriel, hoping that

all your wishes will come true

– G.S.

For the Grandpas: Grandpa Peter

and Grandpa Michio

– R.R.

First published 2012 by Macmillan Children's Books
an imprint of Pan Macmillan.
20 New Wharf Road, London N1 9RR
Associated companies throughout the world
www.panmacmillan.com

ISBN: 978-0-230-75816-2 (HB)
ISBN: 978-0-230-75817-9 (PB)

Text copyright © Gillian Shields 2012
Illustrations copyright © Rosie Reeve 2012
Moral rights asserted.

5 7 9 8 6 4

A CIP catalogue record for this book is available from the British Library.

Printed in China

Gillian Shields

Rosie Reeve

WILLIAM'S WINTER WISH

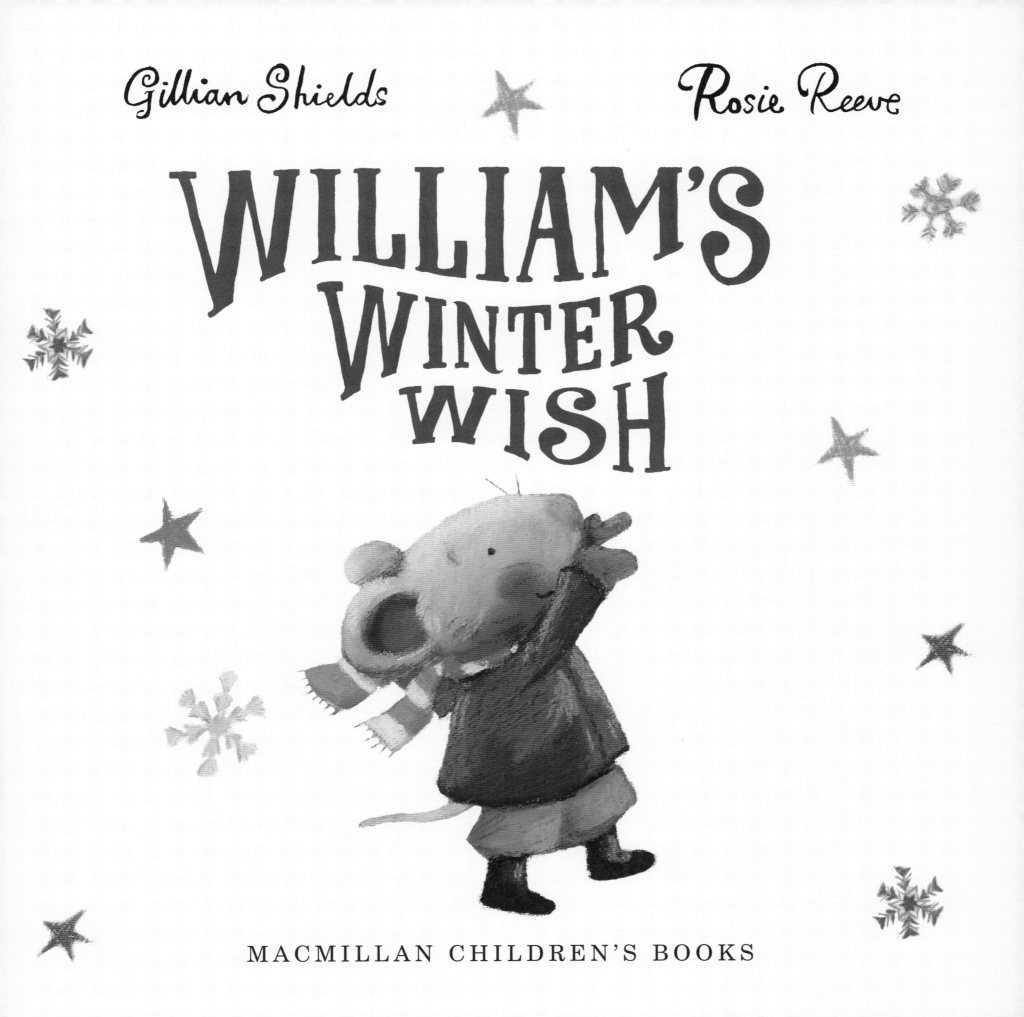

MACMILLAN CHILDREN'S BOOKS

William loved visiting Grandpa's house.
There were lots of wonderful things there:
a cuckoo clock, a train set and a tin of
chocolate biscuits, especially for William.

But the thing William loved best was Grandpa's snow globe. It was round and heavy, and full of tiny snowflakes, which sparkled like magic.

One cold and windy day, William looked out of Grandpa's window. "If only it would snow," he sighed.

"Did it snow when you were little, Grandpa?" he asked. "Every winter," Grandpa replied, reaching for his photo album. "Ooh, show me!" said William, snuggling up.

"Well, when the snow was thick, we threw snowballs and made a snowmouse with a funny nose," smiled Grandpa.

"And when the world froze all glittery and white, we skated across the pond. You would have loved it, William!"

"Can you make it snow now, Grandpa?" asked William. "Please!" Grandpa laughed kindly. "Why don't you make a wish on the snow globe?" he suggested, handing it to William.

William shook and shook, until the snow danced and swirled inside the glass. "I wish that it would really snow," he said.

"I wish!

I wish!

I wish!"

But it didn't snow, not that day or the next, though
William couldn't stop hoping that it would.

He went sledging down the stairs.
"Careful!" said Mum.

He skated on the kitchen floor.
"Oh, William!" sighed Mum.

And he even found some soft,
feathery snowflakes to play with.

"That's it, William," groaned Mum. "Outside!"

William went into the garden and started to play with some old boxes.

When his friends passed by, they stared in surprise. "What are you doing?" they asked.

"Making a snowmouse, of course!" said William. "Do you want to help?"

"But there isn't any snow!" they laughed. "You are funny!" William felt cross. "I'll show them!" he thought. "It *will* snow! I just need to wish harder."

So he hurried over to Grandpa's house.

"Hello, William!" said Grandpa. "Come in and I'll fetch the biscuit tin. I've got some of your favourites."

As Grandpa went into the kitchen, William couldn't wait, not even for a minute. He had to make another wish. This time, he'd wish so hard he would burst!

William stretched up to the snow globe, and . . .

...CRASH!

It fell and broke into a million pieces.

"I'm so sorry, Grandpa!" cried William.

"It doesn't matter," said Grandpa. "It was only an accident."

But William could tell Grandpa was sad. He burst into tears and ran home to his mum.

"I wish I hadn't touched the snow globe!" William sobbed. "Grandpa's unhappy now." "Perhaps you can do something to make him feel better," said Mum gently.

William thought hard, then went to find his piggy bank. He'd been saving to buy a toy, but now he had a better idea. "Can we go to the shops, Mum?" he asked.

William looked in all the shops until he found just what he wanted. The shopkeeper wrapped it up in a parcel. "Carry it carefully," he said with a smile.

MICE CREAM

"I'll be extra careful," William promised.

William rushed straight to see
Grandpa. "Surprise!" he said.
"I got you a present, to say sorry.
Do you like it?" asked William,
excitedly. "Do you?"

It was a new snow globe, even more beautiful than the old one. "I love it!" said Grandpa, giving William a hug. "Thank you! Now, why don't we make one more wish together?"

They shook and shook, until tiny snowflakes fell in the glass, all glittery and white. "I know what I'm wishing for!" squeaked William.

The next morning, William woke to a magical world of white. Sparkling flakes of snow were falling everywhere, just like in Grandpa's snow globe. "My wish came true!" shouted William. "It's snowing!"

He grabbed his scarf and mittens, and
ran out into the glittering, wintery world.

William and his friends
played all day in the snow.
They threw snowballs . . .

and slipped and slid on the ice.

Then they made a snowmouse
with the funniest nose.
"I told you it would snow!"
laughed William.

When it was time to go home,
Grandpa arrived with a surprise for
William – a beautiful, shiny sledge!

They swooshed down the
hill together, all the way
back to Grandpa's house.

Mum was waiting for them with mugs of frothy hot chocolate and a cosy fire. "Will it snow every winter now, Grandpa?" William asked. Grandpa gazed at the snow globe. "Well, if it doesn't," he smiled, "all you have to do is wish!"

William sighed happily. "I do love the snow," he said. "But there's something I love even more."
"What's that?" asked Grandpa.
"YOU!" laughed William.